Little Ant
and the Wasp

S.M.R. Saia

Illustrations by Tina Perko

Every year, ants from all over the field competed against each other to play Kick the Crumb. The anthill that won the tournament was considered to be the best anthill of all.

Every ant wanted to try out for the team. The queen asked their friend the wasp to come and be in charge of the tryouts because she knew the wasp was both tough and fair.

Little Ant was excited. I am stronger than I was last year, Little Ant thought to himself. I am quicker than ever too. I will certainly make the team this year.

Buddy Ant also tried out every year, but Buddy Ant was not as strong or as quick as Little Ant. "The ants who were on the team last year are sure to be on the team again this year," Buddy Ant said nervously, "so there probably aren't very many spaces open."

"We will both make the team," Little Ant said to his friend. But deep down inside, in a place that Little Ant didn't want to admit was there, he hoped that if only one of them could make the team, that it would be him, and not Buddy Ant.

The day for the tryouts finally arrived. Many ants showed up, and only twelve could be on the team. Little Ant looked at them all. That ant is not as fast as me, he thought. That ant does not kick as far as me. That ant almost always misses the goal. I am better at Kick the Crumb than all of these ants, Little Ant decided. There is no way that I will not make the team.

"The first stage of the tryouts will be running," the wasp told them. "I will divide you into groups of ten. The fastest five out of every group of ten will move on to the second stage of the tryouts."

Little Ant was very pleased with his group. He knew he could run much faster than any of them, including Buddy Ant.

When it was his group's turn to run, and the wasp buzzed for them to start, Little Ant started running as fast and as hard as he could.

Soon, though, he realized that he did not have to run very fast or very hard to stay out in front, so he only ran fast enough to be the first ant to cross the finish line.

Buddy Ant, running hard and giving it everything he had, was ant number five. "I passed the first stage!" Buddy Ant said joyously.

"I knew you could do it," Little Ant said. But he couldn't help noticing how hard Buddy Ant had to work just to be number five, and he felt very good about how easy it had been for himself to be number one.

"The next stage will be a race too," the wasp said. "But this time, instead of just running, you will race from the starting line to the finish line while kicking a crumb."

The wasp once again divided all of the ants into groups of ten. This time, there were half as many groups as there had been before.

When it came time for his group to race, Little Ant once again looked around at his competition and felt very confident. None of these other ants were as good at running while kicking a crumb as Little Ant.

The wasp gave each of them a crumb. When she buzzed for them to start, Little Ant easily shot off down the field, kicking his crumb. Far behind him, Buddy Ant ran and kicked as hard as he could.

Again, Little Ant was the first across the finish line. Again, Buddy Ant, sweaty and out of breath, was number five.

"Tomorrow, there will be two games of Kick the Crumb," the wasp told them. "After both games, I will choose the ants who will play for your anthill at this year's tournament. Rest up tonight, and be back here first thing in the morning, ready to try your hardest!"

"Let's practice passing the crumb back and forth while we run down the field," Buddy Ant suggested.

"I'm tired," Little Ant said. "I think I should rest up for tomorrow, like the wasp said. Come back to the anthill with me instead."

"No," Buddy Ant said. "I was the fifth ant to cross the finish line in both races. I am going to practice so I can do a good job in the game tomorrow."

Buddy Ant was not the only ant who wanted to practice. Soon, a small group of ants were running up and down the field, kicking the crumb back and forth between them. Little Ant relaxed and watched them.

Buddy Ant ran harder than any other ant. He kicked harder than any other ant. He tried harder than any other ant to get the crumb. Sometimes he succeeded. Sometimes he didn't.

Buddy Ant tries very hard, Little Ant thought to himself, but he is not very good at Kick the Crumb. Soon, Little Ant got bored and fell asleep.

The next day, Little Ant and Buddy Ant found out that their team would not be the first to play. "Let's watch the first game, Buddy Ant," Little Ant suggested.

"I don't think so, Little Ant," Buddy Ant said. "I am going to use this extra time to practice."

So Little Ant watched the first game while Buddy Ant practiced kicking the crumb into the space between two dandelions. Sometimes the crumb went into the goal. Sometimes it didn't.

When it was time for their game, Little Ant felt confident. When his team began to move the crumb down the field toward the goal, Little Ant ran out ahead of the other ants. He ran so fast that there was no other ant near him, and he was close enough to the goal to score. Where was the crumb?

Then he saw Buddy Ant, surrounded by ants from the other team. Buddy Ant was struggling to hang on to the crumb and keep it moving down the field.

"Buddy Ant!" Little Ant cried. "Over here! I'm open! Kick the crumb to me!"

Buddy Ant kicked the crumb to Little Ant, and Little Ant dribbled the crumb toward the goal. The ants from the other team ran their hardest to catch him. Little Ant waited until they had almost caught up to him before he kicked the crumb into the goal. He looked over his shoulder to make sure the wasp had seen him. Scoring this goal will get me a place on the team for sure, Little Ant thought smugly.

But when both games were over, and the wasp announced who would be on the team, she did not call Little Ant's name.

"Why didn't you put me on the team?" Little Ant asked the wasp. "I was the fastest ant on the field."

"You may have been the fastest," the wasp said, "but you did not try the hardest. Whatever you do, Little Ant, you should do with all your might. You did not race with all your might yesterday, and you did not play with all your might today."

Not far away, the ants who had made the team were celebrating. Little Ant went up to them. "Congratulations, Buddy Ant," he said.

"I can't believe I made the team!" Buddy Ant said. "I am not the fastest ant. I don't always kick straight enough or hard enough."

"But you try harder than any other ant on the field," Little Ant told him. "You deserve to be on the team. I am very proud of you, Buddy Ant."

Little Ant's anthill did not win the tournament that year, but Little Ant enjoyed the game more than any other he had ever watched. Whenever Buddy Ant had the crumb, sometimes he got it farther down the field,

and sometimes he didn't. When Buddy Ant kicked the crumb, sometimes it went where he wanted it to, and sometimes it didn't. But the harder Buddy Ant tried, the better he got, and Little Ant cheered him on with all of his might.

Copyright 2021 by S.M.R. Saia
Illustrations by Tina Perko

Free activities for the Little Ant books are available at
http://littleantbooks.com.

All rights reserved. No part of this book may be reproduced or used in any manner whatsoever without the express written permission of the publisher.

Published by Shelf Space Books
http://shelfspacebooks.com

ISBN: 978-1-945713-34-7

CPSIA information can be obtained
at www.ICGtesting.com
Printed in the USA
LVHW071745171221
706475LV00030B/2869